Bo the Brave

Read more
UNICORN DIARIES
books!

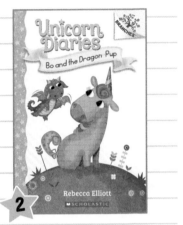

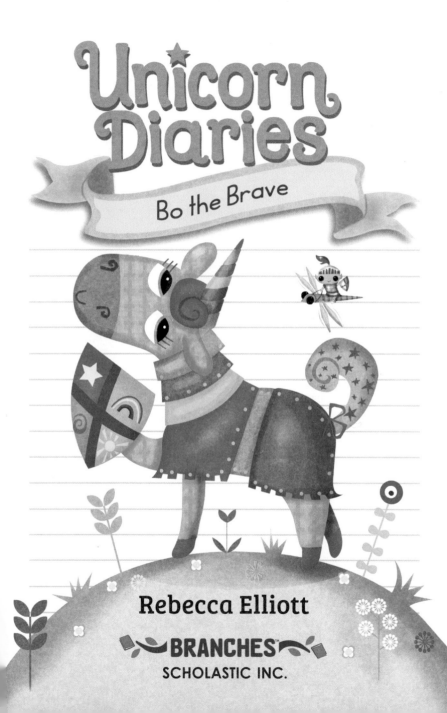

Unicorn Diaries

Bo the Brave

Rebecca Elliott

BRANCHES
SCHOLASTIC INC.

For my Mum. A truly magical being. X —R.E.

Special thanks to Kyle Reed
for his contributions to this book.

Copyright © 2020 by Rebecca Elliott

All rights reserved. Published by Scholastic Inc., *Publishers since 1920.*
SCHOLASTIC, BRANCHES, and associated logos are trademarks
and/or registered trademarks of Scholastic Inc.

The publisher does not have any control over and does not assume
any responsibility for author or third-party websites or their content.

No part of this publication may be reproduced, stored in a retrieval system,
or transmitted in any form or by any means, electronic, mechanical,
photocopying, recording, or otherwise, without written permission of the
publisher. For information regarding permission, write to Scholastic Inc.,
Attention: Permissions Department, 557 Broadway, New York, NY 10012.

This book is a work of fiction. Names, characters, places, and incidents are
either the product of the author's imagination or are used fictitiously, and any
resemblance to actual persons, living or dead, business establishments,
events, or locales is entirely coincidental.

Library of Congress Cataloging-in-Publication Data

Names: Elliott, Rebecca, author.
Title: Bo the brave / Rebecca Elliott.
Description: New York : Branches/Scholastic, 2020. | Series: Unicorn Diaries; 3 |
Summary: In order to earn their Bravery Patches, Bo and the other unicorns of
Sparklegrove Forest have to camp out in the forest for three nights; but
the night is full of frightening noises, and when a misunderstanding
offends some pixies, the unicorns resolve to face their fears and
confront the "monsters" who are stealing the pixies' houses.

Identifiers: LCCN 2019038828 | ISBN 9781338323429 (paperback) |
ISBN 9781338323436 (library binding) | ISBN 9781338323443 (ebk)
Subjects: LCSH: Unicorns–Juvenile fiction. | Magic–Juvenile fiction. |
Courage–Juvenile fiction. | Camping–Juvenile fiction. |
Pixies–Juvenile fiction. | CYAC: Unicorns–Fiction. | Magic–Fiction. |
Courage–Fiction. | Fear of the dark–Fiction. | Camping–Fiction. |
Pixies–Fiction.
Classification: LCC PZ7.E45812 Bm 2020 | DDC [Fic]–dc23
LC record available at https://lccn.loc.gov/2019038828

10 9 8 7 6 5 4 3 2   20 21 22 23 24

Printed in China   62
First edition, July 2020

Edited by Katie Carella
Book design by Maria Mercado

Table of Contents

Glitterrific Greetings!

Sunday

Hello, lovely Diary!
It's your favorite unicorn – Rainbow Tinseltail! But everyone calls me Bo.

I live in an enchanted wood called Sparklegrove Forest.

Here it is! It's a **TWINKLE-TASTIC** place to live.

Rainbow Falls

Troll Caves

Glimmer Glade

Sparklegrove School for Unicorns

Dragon Nests

Budbloom Meadow

Snowbelle Mountain

Unipods

Fairy Village

Twinkleplop
Lagoon

Goblin
Castle

We share this forest with other
magical creatures . . .

Like pixies! Here are four fun facts about pixies:

Tree Sprite

Pixie

Fairy

They're the smallest creatures in the forest. (They're even smaller than fairies and tree sprites!)

They live in tiny, shiny houses.

They wear armor and fly around on dragonflies.

EEK!

They're very easily scared.

As you already know, <u>I'm</u> a unicorn!

Horn
Every unicorn's horn is different!

Eyes
Big and twinkly!
We can see things
a long way away.

Rainbow Mane
We can keep stuff in it!
(And it looks pretty!)

Tail
Swishing it makes our Unicorn Power
work. It's also fun to braid!

Unicorns are MUCH more than a colorful horn though. Here are some **GLITTERRIFIC** facts:

We each have a different Unicorn Power. I'm a Wish Unicorn.

I can grant one wish every week!

We glow when we're nervous or scared.

Our horns are great for scratching
one another's backs.

We're not very good at math.
(Actually, that might just be me.)

2+6=???

I live with my friends at Sparklegrove School for Unicorns. S.S.U. is the BEST!

Here's my BEST friend, Sunny. He can turn invisible!

Sunny Huckleberry

Crystal-Clear Unicorn

My other friends have cool Unicorn Powers, too.

Nutmeg Silvertips

Flying Unicorn

Scarlett Sugarlumps

Thingamabob Unicorn

Jed Glitterock

Weather Unicorn

Monty Dumpling

Size-Changer Unicorn

Piper Forestine

Healer Unicorn

Mr. Rumptwinkle

our teacher

Shape-Shifter Unicorn

At S.S.U., we study **SUPER-SPARKLY** subjects like:

GLITTER PAINTING

HISTORY OF SPARKLEGROVE FOREST

HISTORY

MAGICAL STORYTELLING

Once upon a magical time . . .

USE OF UNICORN POWERS

My friends and I each have a special unicorn patch blanket. Every week, we try to earn a new patch.

These patches show everything I've learned so far.

I can't wait for Mr. Rumptwinkle to decide what this week's patch will be!

Spooky Stories

Diary,

Sorry if my writing is a bit wobbly, but I'm a bit scared! Last night, Jed told us a bedtime story and, well, it was a bit <u>spooky</u>!

It was a dark and stormy night in the forest . . .

After he finished his story, we left our horns glowing all night because we were feeling afraid of the dark. (Even Jed was scared!)

Then, just as we had calmed down
enough to sleep, Monty screamed!

He'd spotted a big spider running
through our **UNIPOD**! This made us all
jump! But the spider was only. . .

You will camp outside for three nights.

Will you be there?

No.

Oh.

But there's nothing to be scared of in Sparklegrove Forest. We've studied its creatures and its history. Plus, you'll be together! There will be four of you in one tent, and three in the other.

We were excited AND a bit scared to camp out on our own.

I can't wait to get my BRAVERY patch!

Camping is going to be fun.

Yes, but the forest is so dark at night.

We've got our powers – and one another!

As long as we stick together, we'll be fine.

I hope I'm right, Diary! Whatever happens, this will be an adventure!

A Dark and Stormy Night

Tuesday

We spent the morning packing for our campout.

Then, we trotted to Budbloom Meadow.

We set up our tents.

We built a fire.

And we ate dinner.

This is fun!

It's not scary at all!

But it will be dark soon.

19

When the stars came out, we got into our tents. I felt nice and cozy with Sunny, Piper, and Monty nearby.

We were all feeling pretty brave
until –

Suddenly, our tent flap flew open!

Jed, Scarlett, and Nutmeg ran into our tent. They looked just as scared as we felt.

Can we stay in here with you?
Good idea.
But maybe if we want to earn our BRAVERY patch, we shouldn't hide. Shouldn't we try to find out what that noise is?
Yeah . . . But what if something really scary is making those sounds?
Then, we'll face it together.

We knew we would need to be VERY brave if we were going to find out what that noise was. So we came up with a plan.

Scarlett used her thingamabob power to create a powerful flashlight.

Using their powers, Monty became small and Sunny turned invisible. This way, they could sneak around outside without being seen.

We shone the flashlight out of the tent flap so Monty and Sunny could see as they searched around our tents.

They didn't find anything or anyone.

Just then, we heard the noise again!

THUMP!...THUMP!...EEK!
THUMP!...THUMP!...EEK!

We all galloped back inside to hide.

What do we do now?!

I had an idea!

Jed, you could use your power to make it rain. A thunder-and-lightning storm might scare away whatever is out there.

Good plan!

So Jed made it storm for the rest of the night.

And it worked! We didn't hear any more scary noises! (Or was that because of the loud, scary thunder?) Either way, we hardly got any sleep!

4

Let's All Be Brave

This morning, we felt SO tired.

Now that the sun is shining, nothing seems scary.

And the noises have definitely stopped.

But <u>something</u> made those noises last night.

We slept most of today so we could be ready to face our fears tonight.

Soon, it was nighttime. We all stood bravely outside our tents waiting for the noises to begin again.

We waited. And waited. Then suddenly –

Monty made himself giant (in case there was a huge monster waiting for us!). My heart was beating so loudly, I thought the whole forest could hear it!

We came to a big bush.

Monty looked over the bush and started laughing.

We climbed through the bush until we finally saw what had been making the noises . . .

Pixies!!!! They were having a party! The thump thump sound was their drums and the squeaky eek sound was their singing!

Hello, unicorns!

We're having our midsummer celebration.

EEK!

THUMP

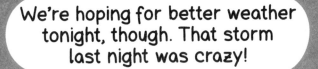

We're hoping for better weather tonight, though. That storm last night was crazy!

PIXIES?!? We'd been scared of PIXIES?!

THUMP!

THUMP!

EEK!

EEK!

EEK!

THUMP!

We all started laughing SO hard that our bellies hurt! Some of us even fell to the ground!

Then, Sunny accidentally rolled over the pixies' houses!

But Sunny falling over had made Jed, Scarlett, and Nutmeg laugh <u>even</u> <u>more</u>.

That's when the rest of us realized the pixies <u>weren't</u> laughing with us. They actually looked a bit upset.

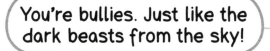

You're bullies. Just like the dark beasts from the sky!

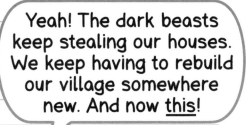

Yeah! The dark beasts keep stealing our houses. We keep having to rebuild our village somewhere new. And now <u>this</u>!

Before we could say anything, the pixies flew away!

BEASTS FROM THE SKY?! What beasts??

When the others stopped laughing, we told them what the pixies had said about the "beasts from the sky."

Oh, I'm sure there's nothing to be afraid of. You know pixies get scared super easily.

I still can't believe <u>we</u> were scared by pixies!

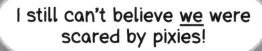

I don't think you should have laughed so much though. Not after their houses got wrecked. They were really upset.
We weren't laughing at them. We were only laughing at ourselves.

I think the pixies were right: You were kind of being bullies.
We are NOT bullies!
And if you think we are, then maybe we'll go camp somewhere else tonight.
Fine.
FINE.

So Jed, Nutmeg, and Scarlett moved their tent to the other side of Budbloom Meadow.

Oh, Diary, I don't feel scared anymore. But now I feel sad for the pixies and their houses AND I'm sad we've fallen out with our friends.

5

RUN!

Thursday

I woke up this morning feeling terrible about the fight with Jed, Nutmeg, and Scarlett.

Come on. Let's go make up with them.

Then we can find the pixies and say "sorry" to them again, too.

Yes. We need to make things right.

Let's do it!

We galloped across the meadow.
But our friends weren't in their tent!

We searched until it got dark. But
we couldn't find them anywhere!

Should we tell Mr. Rumptwinkle what happened?
Yes! Maybe he can help us find them.
I think we should be brave and try to solve this mystery on our own.
You're right! Let's make a plan.

We ducked into our tent. All of a sudden, Piper turned pale.

Uh-oh. I think I know what happened to them . . . It must be the BEASTS that the pixies were talking about!

The BEASTS FROM THE SKY have taken our friends?!

This never would've happened if we'd stayed together. We need to find them!

We knew we had to go out into the dark forest. But we were nervous.

My tail swirled as I used my Unicorn Power. Soon, we were wearing armor!

If there are beasts out there, we are ready for battle!

I'm sorry our armor is not shiny like the pixies' armor. But it is strong.

We marched into the forest feeling very brave.

That is, until we heard something moving in the trees above us.

It must be the giant beasts!

They're chasing us!

RUN!

We galloped at full speed. But the rustling sound followed us.

Then, we heard voices coming from a
nearby cave.

We found Scarlett, Jed, and Nutmeg
inside!

We're so glad you're okay!

The beasts didn't get you after all!

We went for an early morning trot, but something up in the trees chased us into here.

We think it's the beasts the pixies told us about.

That's what we think, too!

54

We stayed in the cave all night, and everyone apologized. Scarlett, Jed, and Nutmeg said sorry for laughing at the pixies. And we said sorry for calling them bullies.

I feel so happy we're all friends again. But on the other **HOOF**, I feel <u>so</u> scared that there are beasts out there!

Battle the Beasts!

Friday

This morning, we knew we had to make things right with the pixies AND earn our BRAVERY patch.

Come on! Let's find the pixies!

We trotted around until we heard a familiar sound.

When we found the pixies, we all said a big "sorry" to them.

We thought there were big, scary creatures that we were going to have to fight. We were just <u>so</u> relieved when we saw you that we started giggling.

And I'm so sorry for breaking your houses. I didn't mean to.

We know it was an accident.

Besides, since the beasts often take our houses, we're good at making new ones.

Then, we heard the rustling noise again in the trees above us! The pixies hid behind us.

We were SO scared, but we tried to be brave for the pixies. And then guess what flew down from the trees?

Magpies!

We smiled as we shooed the birds away.

It's safe now!

Your "beasts from the sky" are only magpies!

Those birds just like to collect shiny things. They love adding a little sparkle to their nests.

So they keep taking our houses just because they're <u>shiny</u>?

Yes.

Wait a minute! I have an idea to help you.

Scarlett used her thingamabob power to pull coins from her mane.

Let's try to get the magpies to take these shiny coins instead of your houses!

If only your houses were less shiny, too.

HMMM.

I have just the thing for building strong, <u>non</u>-shiny houses — unicorn armor!

We helped the pixies remake their houses. They looked so cute!

And when the magpies came back, they loved the shiny coins!

Then, the pixies asked us to join them for the last night of their midsummer celebration!

Time to party!

We were worried we wouldn't get our BRAVERY patch. After all, we hadn't battled any scary monsters and we'd all been scared AND had hidden in a cave.

We had the Patch Parade right there at the pixie party!

Then it was time to say good-bye.

7
We Partied Like Pixies

After the party, we headed back to school. We were SO tired by the time we got to our **UNIPOD**!

Well, Diary, this week has been such an adventure! But being brave sure is tiring . . . Even unicorn knight heroes need their sleep! Goodnight!

Rebecca Elliott may not have a magical horn or sneeze glitter, but she's still a lot like a unicorn. Rebecca always tries to have a positive attitude, she likes to laugh a lot, and she lives with some great creatures — her guitar-playing husband, her noisy-yet-charming children, her lovable but naughty dog Frida, and a big, lazy cat called Bernard. She gets to hang out with these fun characters and write stories for a living, so she thinks her life is pretty magical!

Rebecca is the author of several picture books, the young adult novel PRETTY FUNNY, the Unicorn Diaries early chapter book series, and the bestselling Owl Diaries series.

Unicorn Diaries

How much do you know about Bo the Brave?

Many magical creatures live in Sparklegrove Forest, including pixies. What are two fun facts about pixies? Reread page 4.

Reread page 31. "Knights" and "nights" are homophones. These words sound the same, but are spelled differently and have different meanings. What are the meanings of "knights" and "nights"?

Why are the pixies scared of the magpies?

There are many ways to be brave. Being brave can mean camping in the dark, but it can also mean standing up to your friends or saying you're sorry. Draw a picture of a time when you felt brave.

Jed tells a spooky story that begins with "It was a dark and stormy night in the forest..." What happens next? Write your own spooky story!